DINOSA
VALENTiNE

by Liza Donnelly

Cartwheel
·B·O·O·K·S·™

SCHOLASTIC INC.

New York   Toronto   London   Auckland   Sydney

Love,
Grandma
Truban
Jan. 2010

For Gretchen

With special thanks to Dr. William Gallager of the New Jersey State
Museum and William Seldon of the Rutgers Geology Museum
for fact checking the glossary.

A LUCAS • EVANS BOOK

No part of this publication may be reproduced in whole or in part, or stored in a retrieval
system, or transmitted in any form or by any means, electronic, mechanical, photocopying,
recording, or otherwise, without written permission of the publisher. For information
regarding permission, write to Scholastic Inc., 730 Broadway, New York, NY 10003.

ISBN 0-590-46415-9

12 11 10 9 8 7 6 5 4 3 2 1   4 5 6 7 8 9/0

Printed in the U.S.A.   24

First Scholastic printing, January 1994

"These dinosaur valentines are great, Bones! Let's go out and give them to some of our favorite people."

"Did you know, Bones, that a Montanoceratops would not have been friends with a Cellosaurus because they lived in different times?"

"Happy Valentine's Day, Ms. Paley!"

"But a Scutellosaurus might give a valentine to a Cetiosaurus, if they liked each other of course! They both lived in the Jurassic period."

"Happy Valentine's Day, Mr. Pisano!"

"And a Struthiosaurus might give a valentine to you, Mrs. Givens, if you lived in the Cretaceous period!"

"Wouldn't it be fun, Bones, to be able to give a valentine
to a dinosaur? Which dinosaur do you like best, Bones?"

"Bones? Where did you go, Bones??"

"There you are! What's that?"

"It's an invitation to a party, a Valentine party! Where did you find this, Bones?"

"Look, Bones. Isn't that an Othnielia?"

"Hey! Come back! You've got a dinosaur in there!"

"Hey wait!"

"You sneak around and lure the dog catcher, Bones, and I'll free the Othnielia."

*"Thank you! That was quite a ride! Did you get my invitation? Are you going to the party?"

*"Happy Valentine's Day, Rex and Bones!!"

"What a great party. You are all friends, aren't you?"

"And we want to be your friends, too."

"Look, it's the dog catcher again! Run!"

"Wow!"

"I guess we should go now, Bones."

"Good-bye! Thank you for the party!!"

"You got a valentine, Bones. Let's read it."

"Roses are red
   Violets are blue
   Happy Valentine's Day
   To you!
        From your pal Othnielia"

GLOSSARY

CETIOSAURUS (SEE-tee-o-sawr-us). *Whale lizard.* Weighing up to ten tons, this large dinosaur measured 50 to 60 feet long. The name *whale lizard* refers to its great size, not to any ocean life. Cetiosaurus was a plant-eater.

CELLOSAURUS (SELL-o-sawr-us). *Cell lizard.* Lightly built, this dinosaur had a long body and long fingers. It measured only eight feet long. It could grasp plants to eat, particularly with the help of its thumbs.

LEPTOCERATOPS (lep-toe-SAIR-uh-tops). *Delicate horned face.* Named for its slender build, this plant-eater was seven feet long and could have walked on two legs as easily as four. It had a neck frill and a parrot-like beak for cutting tough leaves and twigs. Leptoceratops had a paddle-like tail possibly used for swimming.

MONTANOCERATOPS (mon-TAN-o-sair-uh-tops). *Montana horned face.* This plant-eater had one horn on its face and a frill on its neck. It was named for the state of Montana, where it was found. Ten feet long, it could walk on its hind legs but spent most of its time browsing on all fours.

OTHNIELIA (oth-NEEL-ee-ah). This dinosaur was named in honor of Othniel Charles Marsh, the scientist who discovered it. A plant-eater, Othnielia was only four feet long, light weight, and a fast runner. It may have lived in herds and is sometimes called the gazelle of the dinosaur world.

PISANOSAURUS (pee-SAN-o-sawr-us). *Pisano's lizard.* This primitive dinosaur had three different kinds of teeth. It ate plants and walked on two legs. Three feet long, it was probably a very fast runner.

SCUTELLOSAURUS (scoo-TELL-o-sawr-us). *Little shield lizard.* The only armored dinosaur of its kind, Scutellosaurus gets its name from the rows of bony studs on its back. This dinosaur was just four feet long. It had a very long tail and a light weight body.

STRUTHIOSAURUS (STROOTH-ee-o-sawr-us). *Harsh lizard.* The smallest dinosaur of its type, this plant-eater was six to seven feet long. Struthiosaurus had plates around its neck, bony studs on its tail, and a fringe of spikes on its side. It had a birdlike skull.

IGUANODON (ee-GWAN-o-don). *Iguana-tooth.* Thirteen feet in length, the bulky Iguanodon was probably not a good runner. It browsed slowly for low-lying plants, but could rear up on all fours to reach higher plants or to escape a predator.